SPECIAL COLLECTOR'S EDITION

Adapted from the film by
Anne Mazer
and Lucy Dahl

Based on the motion picture from Walt Disney Pictures
Screenplay by John Hughes
Produced by John Hughes and Ricardo Mestres
Directed by Stephen Herek

Disney
PRESS
New York

Disney's 101 DALMATIANS

SPECIAL COLLECTOR'S EDITION

Printed in the United States of America.

FIRST EDITION
1 3 5 7 9 10 8 6 4 2

Storyboards by Denis Rich.
This book is set in 14-point Berkeley.
Book design by Mara Van Fleet.

ISBN: 0-7868-3118-9 (trade)
ISBN: 0-7868-5045-0 (lib. bdg.)
Library of Congress Catalog Card Number: 96-85929

Based on the book by Dodie Smith, published by Viking Press.

Contents

CHAPTER ONE

Endangered Species

Under a full yellow moon, a tiger perched majestically atop an outcropping of rock. It was alone, the ruler of its domain. As it surveyed its territory, a twig snapped in the dense vegetation behind it. A pale, gaunt man dressed in a black coat, black hat, and black glasses stepped out of the bushes. As he knelt to open his backpack, the moon lit up an ugly scar on his neck.

Lionel Skinner pulled out a rifle equipped with a silencer and scope. The tiger scanned for the enemy he sensed—rather than saw—and Skinner focused on the animal's unusual black-and-white stripes.

With a faint, muffled pop, the rifle fired. The tiger staggered back, then tumbled off the rock.

Skinner rappelled down the rock to where the tiger's lifeless body lay. With his boot, he prodded the animal's stomach, then kneeled and took a black wooden box out of his pack. Inside it lay the instruments of the fur trade. Picking up a long, slender knife, Skinner began his grim work.

He had to work quickly, for he was not in the wild. Skinner had killed an inhabitant of the London Zoo, and it was only a matter of time before its keepers arrived.

In a London bedroom, on a quiet residential street, an alarm clock was ringing loudly. The man in the bed slept through it, as did the Dalmatian on the floor. The old windup clock continued to ring until it tumbled off the edge of the nightstand, bumped the sleeping dog's head, and landed on the floor with a thud. The ringing stopped.

Roger and I are two lovable but quite lonely bachelors. Roger is human. I am a pedigree Dalmatian. My name is Pongo and this is our story.

I jump in quite a bit to tell my side of the story.

A nasty bump on the head first thing in the morning can possibly have two meanings . . . a disastrous day or a remarkable day!

Fortunately, I am a Dalmatian of extremely high intelligence, and I'm not easily irritated by daily dilemmas.

I take care of my pet human,
Roger.

Roger likes to have a shower
every morning . . .
(I prefer to lick myself clean).

He drinks coffee . . .

. . . with milk.

But first, I have to get him out of bed.

Our communication skills are quite sophisticated—

ONE BARK . . . WAKE UP!

TWO BARKS . . . TIME FOR A WALK!

THREE BARKS . . . HURRY UP WITH MY DINNER!

Dogs must never expect their humans to understand them. Humans do understand, however, that a wagging tail means that we are pleased, which is particularly clever, as they themselves do not have a tail to wag. We can also expect complete understanding when it comes to a little extra attention, like when I crawl up onto Roger's lap, which is far too small, or when I roll onto my back to have my stomach scratched . . . I like that!

In another London apartment, the tv news blared from the screen:

"... of endangered animals in the wild, but never before has an animal in captivity been slaughtered for its pelt."

In front of the screen, Perdy, a ravishing female Dalmatian, growled and barked angrily.

"Isn't that horrible? Who could do a thing like that?" Anita, Perdy's human, came in from the kitchen, a cup of tea in her hand. She was a slender, lovely young woman in her late twenties.

Perdy whimpered in agreement.

"If the battle to preserve threatened species has moved into the urban zoological park," the reporter continued, "we must ask ourselves if any animal in the world is safe."

A frightened Perdy edged away from the TV screen.

Roger sat on a park bench and read the grim headline, ZOO CAT LOSES STRIPES.

"Another bad day for the animal kingdom," Roger sighed. He rolled up the paper and shoved it under his arm. "I have to get ready for my meeting this afternoon," he said to Pongo. "One day very soon, I'm going to make a sale."

He rose from the bench and picked up Pongo's leash. "We're fast approaching the point where I'm going to have to start eating your table scraps.

"I exaggerated," Roger said. "It's not that bad, but it is important that the meeting goes well, and you know how I am about meetings. I tend to get a little nervous. . . ."

 **R**oger's needs are different from mine. He likes me to listen to him talk. He talks a lot and I understand everything he says to me. After all, I have one of the most extraordinary brains in Dogdom. But I hope he won't eat my scraps!

I take Roger for our daily walk. I let him ride his bicycle so that he can keep up with me.

He reads the newspaper, and I see my friends.

I find it particularly interesting the way humans try to look like their pets.

Terry and his pet are jogging. Both are looking exhausted today—tongues out, sweat dripping off the human's forehead, drool hanging off Terry's tongue!

Here comes Fido. Both he and his human seem to get shorter and fatter every week!

But we're going to Roger's meeting. I'll see my friends later.

CHAPTER 2

The House of De Vil

At the House of De Vil, the well-known fashion house, a doorman came smartly down the steps. "Top of the morning," he said as he opened the door to the black and white Panther De Vil limousine.

A smoldering cigarette in a long holder emerged from the car. With a single tap, an elegant finger knocked off the ash, squarely on the toe of the doorman's newly shined shoe.

A trail of cigarette smoke wafted through the black-and-white lobby, where another doorman stood rigidly at attention. The elevator doors opened and closed, revealing walls painted in black-and-white tiger stripes. The elevator man tried not to cough as the cigarette smoke enveloped him.

In the design studio, Anita bent over her drawing board, sketching a new design for the House of De Vil. The theme was tiger stripes—all the mannequins in the showroom were dressed in black-and-white striped garments in different stages of construction.

"Anita, darling." A cigarette burning in a long holder dangled from the elegant hand of Cruella De Vil. The owner of the House of De Vil was a striking woman with a glacial expression in her eyes.

"Good morning, Cruella," Anita answered.

Cruella glanced down at Anita's drawing board. On it was a flattering sketch of Cruella in a spotted gown. Nervously, Anita slid the drawing under another of the same gown in tiger stripes. Cruella studied it for a moment, then reached forward and moved it so that the two drawings were side by side. Then her eyes shifted to the top of the drawing board, where Anita had taped a photo of Perdy to the top corner. Cruella picked it up. "What a charming dog."

"Thank you," Anita said.

"Spots," Cruella observed. Behind them, the showroom was silent.

"Yes, she's a Dalmatian."

"Inspiration?" Cruella gestured to the spotted gown.

Anita's heart was pounding, but she answered calmly. "Yes."

"Long hair or short hair?"

"Short."

"Coarse or fine?"

"I guess I'd have to say it's a little coarse."

"Pity," Cruella drawled.

"It was very fine when she was a puppy."

"Redemption." With a smile, Cruella returned the photo to the drawing board. "We need to talk."

The doors to the design studio opened. "Ms. De Vil!" Frederick, one of the company's executives, dressed all in black, bustled into the room.

"Come to my office," Cruella told Anita, then hurried off.

As the other designers gazed at Anita in sympathy, she rolled up the drawing, took a deep breath, and rushed after them.

"Lady Ashwell called, desperate for something to wear to meet the American president," Frederick was saying as Anita caught up with them. "You'll recall that she's the rather large woman you had dinner with in December."

"You're being kind," Cruella snapped. "She's enormous. I sat in her shadow all night. Tell her she doesn't need a designer; she needs an upholsterer."

The three arrived at Cruella's office. Her secretary, Alonzo, held open the door. "Tea for me, Alonzo," she ordered as she swept past him into the office.

It was an enormous black-and-white room, which commanded a stunning view of London. The couches were in white leather with black cushions, and the desk, like Cruella's hair, was half black, half white.

Cruella shed her fur into the arms of her young assistant. "Tell me more about these spots," she said, turning to Anita. "I did leopard spots in the Eighties."

"Dalmatian spots are a little different, aren't they?"

"Cozy," Cruella said.

"Cuddly," Anita echoed.

"Classic."

"Less trashy."

"Exactly," Cruella agreed. "Do you like spots, Frederick?"

"I don't believe so, madam," Frederick stammered. "I thought we liked stripes this year."

"What kind of yes-man are you?" Cruella demanded.

Frederick passed a plump hand over his perspiring brow. "What kind of yes-man would you like me to be?"

Cruella ignored him. "Frederick, I'm seeing spots now. What will it cost us to start over on next year's line?"

He shook his head. "Millions."

"Can we afford it?"

"Yes, but . . ."

"Thank you, darling," Cruella said. "Now go away. I have to talk to Anita." She crossed over to her desk and looked at some papers. "Alonzo!" she called imperiously as he came in with the tea. "Did you ask Anita if she'd like something to drink?"

Alonzo gave Anita a panic-stricken look.

"I'm fine, thank you," Anita said hastily. She didn't want him getting in trouble on her account.

"Sit down, please," Cruella ordered her.

Anita perched nervously on the edge of a black leather chair.

"How long have you been working for me?" Cruella asked.

She thought for a moment. "Two years last August."

"You've done wonderful work in that time."

Anita brightened at the unexpected compliment. "Thank you."

"I don't see you socially, do I?"

"No."

Cruella leaned back in her chair and studied Anita. "And you're not very well known, despite your obvious talent."

Anita shrugged. "Notoriety doesn't mean very much to me."

"Until you get a better offer," Cruella said knowingly. "Then we'll see the real Anita."

"I'm happy doing what I'm doing, thank you."

"Your work is fresh and clean, unfettered, unpretentious. It sells. And one of these days, my competitors are going to figure out who you are and they're going to try and steal you away."

Anita sat up straighter. "It never occurred to me to leave my job. For another, anyway."

"What do you mean, 'anyway'?" Cruella said quickly.

"I mean that if I left, it wouldn't be for another job."

"What would it be for?"

"I don't know," Anita said slowly. "If I met someone. If working here didn't fit into our plans."

"Marriage?"

"Perhaps," Anita admitted.

"More good women have been lost to marriage than to war, famine, disease, and disaster. You have talent, darling. Don't squander it."

"I don't think this is something you need to worry about. I have no prospects," Anita said.

"I'm really not surprised."

Anita rose. "I should get back to work."

"Why don't you come to dinner on Friday night?" Cruella asked. "We

can discuss this further."

"I don't like to leave my dog alone in the evening," Anita said. "She's by herself all day."

Cruella stared at her incredulously. "You'd rather have dinner with a dog?"

"It's not a matter of what I'd rather do," Anita tried to explain. "It's more a matter of what I have to do."

Cruella snapped her fingers at Alonzo. "The drawing," she commanded.

Alonzo looked confused.

"Take the drawing from Anita and hand it to me," Cruella snapped. "Is that difficult?"

Alonzo quickly took the drawing from Anita and rushed it over to Cruella. "Thank you," Cruella drawled. "Go stand somewhere until I need you."

Her assistant scurried to a far corner and stood stiffly at attention.

Cruella opened the drawing. "I look wonderful in spots," she murmured. "However, I would like to make one small change." She plucked a pen from the inkwell and, frowning intently, began to rework it.

Anita craned her neck, trying to see what Cruella was doing. "We could do this in linen," she suggested.

"We could do it in any number of materials. It's never the material. It's the pattern." Cruella finished the drawing, then put down her pen and leaned back with a smile. She held the drawing out, then looked at Alonzo and rattled it impatiently. He scurried to the desk to take the drawing and then stood there, waiting for orders.

"Give it to Anita," Cruella ordered.

"Thank you." He hurried to Anita, then looked back at Cruella. "Wait in the corner?"

"Please," Cruella said.

Anita studied the drawing. Cruella had changed the dress into an elegant ankle-length coat. She gazed at her boss in admiration. What talent she had!

Anita laughed to herself. "This is kind of funny." She carefully rolled up the drawing.

"What's that, darling?"

"If we make this coat," Anita said slowly, "it'll be like you're wearing my dog."

Cruella laughed, and her evil laughter continued long after Anita had left her office.

CHAPTER 3

Love at First Sight

Roger sat in front of a large, elegant desk, explaining his latest video game and feeling more nervous every minute. "It's a work in progress," he apologized. "The graphics are very rough."

Behind the desk, a young man nodded in a friendly way to Roger while sipping water from a bottle.

With a burst of renewed confidence, Roger continued his pitch. "Normally, I'd finish the game completely, then bring it to you, but . . ." He paused. "I need the money. I'm on my own now. Freelancing. Without a regular paycheck, money's a little tight."

Allan nodded politely. "I'm not the one you have to convince."

The two men got up and Allan led the way to a back room, where a small, pale nine-year-old was playing Roger's video game with savage concentration.

On-screen, a red ball sailed into a forest. "Fetch!" commanded a voice. An animated Dalmatian bounded after the ball.

Roger and Allan stood in the doorway and watched the kid play. "Herbert's got the best instincts in the industry," Allan explained. "Since he was six, he's picked the top-selling game every year."

Herbert unleashed a rapid succession of joystick shots. At a final bark from the Dalmatian, he leaned back from the monitor.

"What do you think?" Roger asked him eagerly.

He hopped out of the chair and walked over to Roger. "Potentially good graphics, reasonably entertaining premise, the dog's well conceived, the environments are engaging," the kid, who barely reached Roger's waist, rattled off.

Roger broke into a grin.

"But I'm not interested in a game that has

a chubby little dogcatcher as the bad guy," Herbert continued. "Am I a hero because I outrun an overweight government worker?"

He slung a backpack over his skinny shoulder. "Even girls won't like this," he concluded. "Sorry, mate."

"What if it had a better villain?" Roger cried. He had to make a success of this game. "Someone you'd really hate."

"It's not hatred that's important," Herbert informed him. "It's a desire to annihilate."

Tethered to a bicycle rack, Pongo waited patiently for Roger. He wasn't bored, though.

Roger is in a business meeting. He is trying to sell one of our computer games so that he can make some money. Then maybe we can buy a car. I'll keep my paws crossed for him . . . and me!

It is autumn. The leaves are falling from the trees and children are catching them as they gracefully flutter to the ground.

I like autumn.
I like children.
I like puppies.
I LIKE THAT
BEAUTIFUL DALMATIAN THAT
JUST TROTTED PAST!

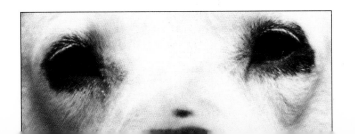

I think she likes me, too!

She looked right at me with those lovely eyes.

She sent a shiver right up my tail!

OH NO! She's walking her human out of sight.

"COME BACK!"

"WAIT! STOP! Please..."

She's gone.
Time to call Roger . . .

"WOOF, WOOF!"
(TIME FOR A WALK)

"WOOF, WOOF!"
(TIME FOR A WALK)

"WOOF, WOOF!"
(TIME FOR A WALK)

"Sorry, Pongo, I didn't know I was going to take so long."

Okay, okay, okay. Now, hurry up, Roger, quickly. Get on your bike. Here we go. Hold on tight. Just hold on . . .

I'll explain later. Just don't fall off!

I must find her. I'll sniff her down. She is the most scrumptious creature I have ever seen. The most delectable dog I have ever smelled. Her long, lovely legs. Her pointed little ears. Her shiny nose . . .

"PONGO, STOP!!!"

Where
did Roger go?

He probably stopped for a rest.

My nose can sniff down a pretty
lady anywhere.

Aha! There she is!
My heart is racing. My eyes are
watering. My ears are twitching.
My legs are weak.

"**P**ongo! What's the matter with you?" Roger tried to turn right, but Pongo veered left, towing the bike and Roger after him. "Pongo!"

They shot down a street, narrowly missing several pedestrians and causing several cars to slam on their brakes.

Roger squeezed the brakes, but they didn't hold. The bike swerved around a corner and into an arcade,

scattering shoppers before them. Then Pongo bounded down a flight of stairs, the bike bumping violently behind him.

Roger screamed as they raced into a crowded intersection and alongside a large red double-decker bus.

Ahead of them, Anita and Perdy turned into St. James's Park. A military band marched toward Pongo and Roger in precise formation. Roger cried out in terror.

Just in time, the soldiers stepped aside. The bike and dog sped past.

The leash ring holding Pongo to the bike strained and then snapped.

Roger screamed as the bike hurtled across a lawn and slammed into a bench. He tumbled off, sailed through the air, and landed with a tremendous splash in the middle of a duck pond.

h no! Watch out, Roger! There's a pond! Uh-oh. He's soaking wet.

A little later, a wet and bedraggled Roger rode his bicycle slowly out of the park. His sweater hung to his knees; one shoe was missing; his flannel pants drooped and sagged. The bike had not fared much better. The frame was twisted into a V. It wobbled and squeaked as he rode it. "Pongo?!" he yelled. He couldn't wait until he got his hands on that dog.

Suddenly he saw him. Pongo was bounding after a ball thrown by an attractive young woman. Roger slowed to a halt and crept after him. Then Roger leaped. "I've got you now!" he cried.

He thinks that lovely lady dog is me! He's got her by the collar—

I'M SO EMBARRASSED!!

I can't look !!

Anita gasped as Roger, holding on to Perdy's collar, stood up, and dragged her toward his bicycle.

"Let go of that dog!" she yelled.

Roger's mouth was set in a thin line. "Stay out of this, lady."

"Stop, or I'll . . . I'll hit you."

"Today is not a good day to threaten me, ma'am."

Anita glared at him. "I don't care if it's a good day or a bad day. . . . I'll hit you nonetheless."

"Whatever," Roger said with a shrug. First the video game, then the bike chase, now this crazy lady.

She pulled her shoulder bag off her arm. "I gave you a proper warning," she said.

Roger sighed. "I've had just about . . ."

She swung, hitting him hard on the head. He went down. "Release my dog or I'll hit you again," she threatened.

The female human is screeching at Roger. I'll just poke my head out a little bit so that he can see there are two of us.

Sorry, Roger. It was like being hit on the head. I had no warning. She just looked at me, and that was that. I was gone. Like falling into a foxhole . . . and . . . and . . . Her name is Perdy. Isn't she beautiful? Exquisite Dalmatian dots. Ravishing . . . I think I'm in love! Sorry again. Of course, all my tail wagging couldn't really tell Roger my story, or my excuses, but I *was* sorry.

Puzzled and groggy, Roger stared at Anita. "Your dog?"

She nodded. "That's my dog. Let her go."

Roger looked closely at Perdy. "He's a she," he said, finally understanding. A familiar canine face peeked out from behind Anita's legs and whimpered.

"Hello, Pongo," Roger said grimly. He released Perdy and stood up. "I beg your pardon, ma'am."

As he put Pongo on his leash, he turned to Anita and asked, "What do you have in that purse of yours? Rocks?"

"Bricks. I'm paving my garden, and every time I see a discarded brick, I pick it up."

"Uh-huh," Roger said. "How many did you find today?"

"Three."

"That's what I would have guessed." He gingerly rubbed the back of his head.

Anita stared at his soggy sweater and dripping pants. "Why are you all wet?"

"I went swimming in the pond," he said sarcastically.

"The water's filthy," she pointed out.

"And it tastes like fish."

"You fell in, didn't you?" she said. "No one with their wits about them swims in a dirty pond in their nice sweater and slacks. And you lost a shoe. Did you know that?"

"As a matter of fact, I did. I noticed it running down the gravel path."

"I'm ever so sorry," she snapped back. "I thought that perhaps if you were silly enough to swim in a pond, you'd be silly enough not to know you'd lost a shoe."

"I crashed my bicycle in the pond," Roger said wearily. "The only part of my body that wasn't injured was my head. But now, thanks to you, I have the complete set of bodily injuries." He held out his hand. "It was nice being assaulted by you, Ms. . . . ?"

"My name's Anita and yours is Roger." She took his hand and shook it. "I read your dog's identification tag."

**Why do humans waste so much time with polite conversation?** Dogs are far more sensible. We sniff each other's noses, followed by a quick bottom sniff.

We never pretend to like anyone. If we do, we lick—and if we don't, we growl. Quite simple, really!

"**N**ice meeting you. I'm very sorry if I alarmed you."

"It's understandable since we both seem to have a certain fondness for Dalmatians," Anita smiled at him.

"And they clearly have a certain fondness for each other."

They gazed down at the two dogs sitting close together.

Roger tugged at Pongo's leash. "Your roving eye has caused me enough trouble today, Pongo," he said. "Let's go home."

Roger wheeled his bike toward home. "You could have gotten me killed, Pongo," he said sternly. "You risked losing your master for a brief frolic with a female."

Pongo hung his head.

"Fools aren't born, Pongo," he lectured. "Pretty girls make them in their spare time." Making sure to keep the leash clear, Roger got on his wrecked bicycle.

Pongo looked around for Perdy. She was trotting next to Anita's bike. The two dogs barked longingly at each other.

"Don't even think about it," Roger warned.

 **wonder if Roger even noticed Perdy's human. She was very pretty and seemed intelligent.**

I can see him thinking. I can always tell when he's thinking, because he starts mumbling, and he becomes quite defensive and reluctant to even acknowledge that he is entertaining the possibility that I might not be entirely wrong.

I think he liked the pretty human. Perhaps he needs another handshake.

"Woof!"

Perdy answered with an excited "woof" of her own.

I definitely wouldn't mind another sniff!!

"Perdy! Stop!" Anita shrieked. Roger jumped off his bike and stared, openmouthed, as Perdy towed Anita's bike at high speed in the direction of the pond. "Look out!" he yelled, running after them, but it was too late.

"You have it entirely wrong, Pongo," Roger said. "I'm simply trying to decide on a route home. It has nothing . . ." He blinked as the sun blinded him momentarily. When he opened his eyes, Anita was gone. ". . . nothing whatever to do with Anita. If that's what her name is." He turned toward home.

CHAPTER 4

A Wedding

An ice bag on his head, a mug of tea in his hands, and a blanket around his shoulders, Roger sat in front of a

think we have a problem," he finally said. "I think my dog's in love."

"I think mine is, too," Anita agreed.

roaring fire in his living room. Next to him, under another blanket, sat Anita. "I've never been rescued before," she said, cradling a hot mug of tea in her hands. "It was very exciting.

There was another silence. Anita sipped at her tea and Roger gazed at the two dogs, who sat beneath a blanket in front of the fire. "I

She turned to look at him. "Why is that a problem?"

"They're going to be brokenhearted when you leave."

The two dogs gazed plaintively at their owners.

"I don't think I can bear to live with a brokenhearted Dalmatian," Anita said softly.

"They're miserable when they're lonely," Roger agreed.

Anita put her cup down. "We

better think of something."

"I agree. Would you like another cup of marriage?"

"Excuse me?" Anita couldn't believe her ears.

"Tea. Another cup of tea?"

"You said marriage," Anita pointed out.

"Marriage?" Roger shifted uncomfortably on the couch.

"That's what you said. You meant to say 'tea,' but it came out 'marriage.'" She smiled at him.

"I'm sorry. Do you want another cup of tea?"

"I do," Anita said.

"You do?"

"I will."

"You will?"

"If you ask me."

Roger gazed nervously into his tea cup. "Would you . . . ?"

"Yes," Anita answered.

Their eyes met. Slowly they moved closer until they kissed. Close to the fire, Pongo and Perdy snuggled happily together.

Anita and Roger faced each other at the altar, their hands joined.

With a subtle shift of his eyes, Roger signaled Anita to look toward the open church doors.

Anita followed the direction of his glance. There stood Pongo and Perdy.

he day Perdy and I were married was the most wonderful day of my life! Roger and Anita had a lovely service for us in a church. They took advantage of our ceremony and exchanged marriage vows at the same time.

All of our friends witnessed our joyous day!

Anita and Roger smiled at each other. "Amen," concluded the minister. Roger lifted Anita's veil and kissed her. Church bells rang.

CHAPTER 5

Jasper and Horace

Its tailpipe belching clouds of gray odorous smoke, the old truck rattled around the corner and pulled to a wheezing stop.

"What's the address?" Jasper hunched over the wheel and peered out the window. He was a tall, gaunt man with bushy eyebrows and small, darting eyes.

"It's slipped my mind, Jasper." Horace's nose was fat; his brain was dull; he hadn't shaved in days.

"You don't have any idea what the number might be?"

Horace struggled to think. "No."

Jasper reached down, grabbed a monkey wrench, and conked him on the head.

"One hundred fifty-two Merton Road, London SW19EH, red-brick town house with a black door," Horace recited rapidly. "You need the telephone number?"

A few minutes later, they were in front of the door.

"Let me tell you about this bloke, Skinner, before we meet him," Jasper warned in a low voice. "When he was quite young, a dog tore open his throat and damaged his vocal chords, leaving him brutally scarred and completely mute. He can't talk at all."

Skinner's tannery was crammed with pelts of all kinds and stuffed and mounted animals and birds. The room reeked of dried blood. Knives and other tools of the fur trade lay on the tables.

"Bloody gruesome line of work you're in, Skinner," Jasper said approvingly.

Horace shuddered.

With a ferocious scowl, Skinner took out a black leather case and thrust it into Jasper's arms.

"Much obliged, sunshine," Jasper said cheerily.

Horace tipped his hat to Skinner, who stared fixedly at his uncovered head. "What?" he asked.

"I think he'd like to turn your nob into a tea cozy."

Slowly Horace backed away from Skinner's weird gaze. The guy was creepy. But Jasper was laughing as if it were a joke.

Out at the truck, Jasper tossed the case on the seat. On the side of the case, a bright sticker proclaimed, I LOVE THE LONDON ZOO.

In her sumptuous bedroom, Cruella sat in bed with a breakfast tray, her correspondence, and the morning paper. As she scanned the society pages, her eyes suddenly narrowed. "How could she do this to me?" she burst out furiously.

She took one more look at the wedding picture of Roger and Anita, Pongo and Perdy; then crumpled up the newspaper and tossed it angrily on the floor.

Alonzo poked his head into the room. "The gentlemen are here."

"Send them in," Cruella ordered, then added nastily, "and fix your hair."

"Morning, ma'am," Jasper said respectfully. He carried the black leather case under one arm. Horace followed him, his mouth hanging open at the opulence of the room.

Cruella waved Alonzo away.

"Lovely day, madam," Jasper said. "Blue skies, birds singing, the laughter of children. It's the kind of day when there wouldn't be an unhappy face in all of London."

"There's one and I'm wearing it," Cruella snapped.

"Fortunately, there's a wicked storm coming in off the Atlantic. . . ." Jasper quickly amended. He patted the case resting on his knees. "I have a little present from Mr. Skinner."

He crossed over to the bed and opened the case. Inside lay the pelt of the tiger Skinner had shot at the zoo.

Cruella's anger disappeared as she pulled the black-and-white fur out of the case. "It's magnificent," she breathed.

She rose with it in her arms and slid it over her shoulders.

"Siberian tiger suits madam very well," Jasper said.

With the fur over her shoulders, Cruella crossed to her dressing room.

40

"Notice, Horace," Jasper said loudly, "how the black-and-white of the wild beast pays homage to madam's own hair-style." He hoped Cruella would hear him.

Horace tugged at his teacup. He had gotten his finger stuck in the handle.

In the dressing room, Cruella modeled the fur before a full-length mirror. Closing her eyes, she stroked it against her face. Jasper watched in alarm as Horace struggled with the teacup.

"Grip it, twist, and yank!" he yelled.

In the other room, Cruella's eyes snapped open. "What?!"

Jasper laughed apologetically. "Just recommending a law firm to my associate here. He's currently with . . ." He glared at Horace. "Hold it, wiggle, and tug."

Horace held the cup with one hand and yanked with the other. His finger popped out. As Jasper watched in horror, the cup slipped from Horace's other hand and flew into the air.

The cup pinged against the ceiling and fell. Horace held out his hat and caught it neatly. The two of them stood frozen as Cruella entered the bedroom.

"What's wrong with you?" Cruella demanded in a harsh voice.

Jasper stared at her. "Nothing."

"Nothing," Horace echoed stupidly.

"You didn't think I was going to pay you?" She smiled nastily and headed toward her desk.

Silently Horace took the cup from his hat, tiptoed over to the tea cart, and replaced it.

Cruella grabbed an envelope full of cash from her desk and pulled out a thick wad of bills. The two men exchanged satisfied glances.

"Now go back to your hovel and wait until I need you again," she commanded.

"I thank you for your continued patronage." Jasper gestured at Horace, who leaned nervously on the tea cart. "As does my associate."

"I do indeed," Horace said, trying to match Jasper in flowery language. "And might I add that you serve a very lovely . . ." He leaned forward for emphasis, ". . . cup of . . ."

Unbalanced by his weight, the tea cart flipped on its back wheels. Horace fell forward, the tea service hurled backward, and teacups and saucers shattered against the wall.

Cruella's eyes glittered with anger. She thrust out her open palm. Jasper slowly put the money back in her hand.

"We'll be at the hovel," he said sadly as he and Horace slunk out of the room.

C H A P T E R   6

More to Come

ur lives as bachelors changed with the arrival of ladies in the house. Everything became calm. Sleeping next to my lovely Perdy is so much nicer than sleeping with Roger. Perdy doesn't snore, nor does she make any of those other distracting—and sometimes smelly—noises that come from Roger.

In her new living room, Anita hung a picture on the wall while Nanny, the housekeeper, dusted the blinds and chattered away happily. "I so loved living with your family when you were little," Nanny confided, "and now to be with you again as you start a family of your own is a dream come true."

Anita shook her head. "I'm not sure Roger and I are quite ready to start a family, Nanny."

"That's a shame. Well, first the puppies, then the babies. . . ."

"Puppies?" Anita stared at her. What was Nanny talking about?

On the second floor, Roger worked on his video game. "If I've done my job right, when this new villain comes on, you're going to run from the room in a panic," he told Pongo.

Pongo's ears pricked up as he watched the screen. An animated Dalmatian ran into a hollow log. Suddenly an evil, slime-dripping dogcatcher, brandishing a net, appeared on-screen.

Roger turned to Pongo, expecting him to bolt in terror. Instead, Pongo yawned. With a sigh of defeat, Roger flipped off the control.

"It's unmistakable, dear," Nanny said to Anita. She pared an apple and put it in a big blue bowl. "You can see it, can't you?"

Anita studied Perdy intently, but she couldn't see anything different about her. Well, she did look unusually contented and happy.

"It's the look every woman gets when she knows she is going to be a mother," Nanny explained. "Notice how tranquil she is? Her eyes are soft and warm."

Unknowingly, Anita's face took on the same expression.

"And though you might not see it," Nanny continued, "you can certainly feel that she's smiling. It's the smile we wear when we're guarding a precious secret."

A quiet smile flitted across Anita's face.

"Now she's living for others as well as for herself. She's eating more."

As if in response to Nanny's words, Anita bit into an apple slice and sighed. Then she leaned over and hugged Perdy. "I think you're right, Nanny," she finally said. "She does look different."

Nanny set down the paring knife and stared as Anita took another slice of apple and smiled sleepily at her.

"What is it, Nanny?"

"Oh, goodness!" Nanny put her hand to her chest. "Anita, dear . . . I think you're going to have a puppy."

Two plus two makes four. Sometimes, if I think about it very hard, it can almost make five . . .

Roger + Anita and Me + Perdy.
2 + 2 = 4

Now, Roger must have thought about it very hard indeed because he tells me that Anita is going to have a baby. And if I'm not mistaken, that will make a definite

five!

Cruella was waiting in the living room as they came back from the doctor's. "Anita! Darling!" she cried, rising dramatically from the couch.

"Cruella!"

She embraced Anita. Suddenly Cruella caught sight of the dogs, cowering behind Roger in the entryway. Her smile faded.

The dogs barked furiously at her.

 **T**he nose of a dog is particularly sensitive and acutely accurate. We can smell the bitter scent of danger through any disguise.

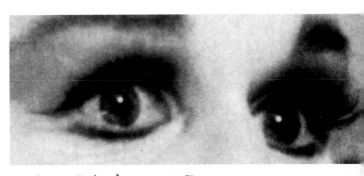

CRUEL(la) DEVIL . . . Her name said it all!

 **Like the day Anita's boss entered our house . . .**

Bitter perfume, cigarette smoke, cosmetics, and the fur of a dead animal. All mixed together to make a revolting, unbearable smell. Her lips were blood red, and her eyes flashed a tinge of the same. I felt her from my nose to my tail. Ferocious, mean, fierce, and bloodthirsty—

She looked at Perdy, and I froze.

I could SMELL this creature from my nose to my tail.

I growled, I snarled, I barked. Roger sent me out of the room for rude behavior. Reluctantly, I obeyed.

(Roger cannot smell trouble . . . just things like bacon cooking and dog droppings in the house!)

Cruella smiled again. "Oh, Anita! Those dazzling dogs!" She nodded curtly to Roger. "You must be Rufus."

Roger stuck out his hand. "It's Roger and it's a pleasure, Ms. De Vil."

"What's a pleasure?" she asked rudely.

"Making your acquaintance," Roger replied.

"Such a sweet thought," Cruella purred. "I wish I could reciprocate." She blew a cloud of smoke in his direction. Ignoring his outstretched hand, she turned to Anita. "Tell me. You married him for his dog."

Anita shot a quick apologetic look toward Roger. He shooed the dogs upstairs and came into the living room.

Cruella swooped onto the sofa. "I've missed you, darling. I hate that you've taken a leave."

"I'm still working," Anita protested. "You've been getting my sketches?"

"It's not the same. I miss the interaction." She turned to Roger. "And what is it that you do that allows you to support Anita in such splendor?"

"I design video games."

"Video games?" Cruella mimicked. "Is he putting me on?"

Anita sprang to Roger's defense. "No. He's very good at it. It's a growing business."

"Those horrible noisy things that children play on their televisions? Someone designs them? What a senseless thing to do with your life."

Roger took a deep breath and changed the subject. "Did Anita tell you the news?" he asked. "She's going to have a baby."

"Is this true?" Cruella demanded.

Anita nodded.

Cruella flicked her cigarette ash on the floor. "You poor thing. I'm so sorry."

"I'm excited about it, Cruella."

Cruella stared at her. "You can't be serious."

"She is," Roger said firmly.

"What can I say?" Cruella sighed. "Accidents will happen."

"We're having puppies, too," Roger said.

Cruella rose and took another drag on her cigarette. "I must say this is somewhat better news. I adore puppies." She turned to Anita. "I will expect a decline in your work product."

"I shouldn't think so," Anita answered.

"Be sure and let me know when the blessed event occurs."

"It won't be for another eight months."

"The puppies, darling." Cruella crossed to the entry and flung open the door. "I have no use for babies," she said.

CHAPTER 7

Puppies and More Puppies!

On a cold rainy autumn afternoon some months later, Roger sat on the living-room couch doing a crossword puzzle. Every few minutes, he glanced at the clock, then at his watch. Finally he rose and crossed to the kitchen door, then looked back at Pongo. "If I'm this nervous about your puppies, what am I going to be like when my baby arrives?" He plunked himself back into the chair. "How can you be so calm?"

The door to the kitchen swung open and Nanny rushed out. Roger and Pongo both jumped up.

"Not yet," Nanny said as she hurried past them.

"What's taking so long?" Roger demanded.

From somewhere upstairs, Nanny yelled, "These things take time!"

Roger sank back into the chair and tried to concentrate on his crossword puzzle. "Four-letter word for 'dome' . . ."

In response, Pongo woofed softly.

"Thank you." Carefully, Roger penciled in the word *roof.*

hen Perdy settled down to have our puppies, I was ready. She had explained to me that she wanted to be alone with Anita when the puppies were being born (my feelings were a little hurt!) and that she had chosen the broom cupboard because it was small, quiet, and safe. She told me that I must remain calm and save my energy for the puppies.

(I always do exactly as Perdy says).

A bolt of lightning flashed through the sky, and thunder rumbled as Jasper and Horace's truck pulled up in front of Roger and Anita's house. "Go peek in the window and see if the puppies have come yet," Jasper ordered.

"It's pouring buckets, Jasper," Horace whined.

"How could I not have noticed?" Jasper said sarcastically.

"Might be you was concentrating on your driving."

"Of course I know it's raining!" Jasper screeched. "Go look in the window."

Horace rubbed his nose. "Have we got an umbrella?"

Reaching down between the seats, Jasper pulled out an umbrella and dumped it on Horace's lap. "Careful when you open it."

With a snap and a whoosh, the umbrella flew open. "Is it bad luck to open an umbrella in a truck?" Horace asked plaintively.

In the kitchen, Anita sat on the floor next to Perdy, gently stroking her head. Suddenly Perdy lay down.

"Nanny!" Anita cried.

Nanny rushed into the kitchen with her arms full of towels. "Gangway!" she yelled.

Horace slid out of the truck and yanked the open umbrella through the door, turning it inside out.

"Now look what you done to my umbrella!" Jasper cried.

Horace shut and then opened it again. The ribs were bent and twisted. "It should be fine now." His mouth dropped open. "I'm sorry Jasper, I forgot what I'm supposed to do."

Jasper grabbed the monkey wrench and conked him on the head.

A brief spark of intelligence flickered in Horace's eyes. "I'll go look in the window and see if them puppies were born yet. And . . . ?"

Jasper gave him another conk.

" . . . run down to the pub and tell the missus if I see any."

"That's right," Jasper growled.

Horace looked confused again. "Why would they have puppies in the pub?"

"The house!" Jasper said. "Look in the window of the house!"

Horace nodded sagely. "For . . . ?"

"Puppies!" Jasper shrieked.

"They're here! The puppies are here!" Nanny cried as she burst into the dining room where Pongo and Roger were waiting.

"You're a father, Pongo!"
That didn't take long!

"You're a father twice!"
Splendid . . . splendid!

"Four . . ."
Terrific!

"Seven . . ."
Steady . . . that'll do.

"Twelve . . ."
We only chose eight names!

FIFTEEN!
Outstanding!!

Fourteen . . . We lost one.
What? Lost one . . . How ridiculous! We must find it!! Look underneath Perdy. I'm sure the little one is not far away. . . .

Oh no . . . You don't mean dead?

Roger, please help. Please! Don't let him die. I promise to take good care of everyone.

I will teach them not to wiz in the house. I won't let them chew your shoes or the furniture. No yapping, I promise . . . and . . . and . . . and . . .

He moved!!! He's breathing!!!

"Fifteen puppies!!!"

Slowly Roger unwrapped the towel to reveal a tiny alert puppy with two black ears and a black circle around one eye.

Roger rose, with the puppy clutched in his arms. "Fifteen!" he called. "We have fifteen puppies!"

Nanny rushed out from the kitchen. "Mercy! Mercy!" She took the puppy from Roger. "We're naming this one Lucky!"

Anita came into the living room.

"How's Perdy?" Roger asked her.

"Tired." Anita didn't look too good herself. Her hair was disheveled and there were dark circles under her eyes.

"Bringing fifteen puppies into the world. I guess she has a right," Roger said sympathetically.

"They're so beautiful." Anita nodded to Pongo, who waited expectantly by the kitchen door. "You can go in, Pongo." She flopped down on a chair with a weary sigh. "I'm glad I'm only having one."

Looking in through the kitchen window, Horace broke into a grin. Then he rushed away in the direction of the pub.

CHAPTER 8

Not for Sale

A triple flash of lightning illuminated the sky as Cruella De Vil marched up to Anita and Roger's house and swept through the front door.

"Anita? Anita!" she cried.

In the living room, Anita cast a frightened look at Roger and jumped to her feet.

"There you are," Cruella snapped. "Where are the puppies?"

Anita stared at her in bewilderment.

"They should have arrived by now," Cruella said impatiently.

Roger stepped forward. "Excuse me!"

Ignoring him completely, Cruella barged into the kitchen. Anita, Roger, and Nanny hurried after her.

Perdy and I were lying quietly with our new puppies. I was delighted with my new family, when quite unexpectedly . . .

she was back!

The fur of a freshly killed animal hung over her shoulders. She glared at our puppies. She wanted them. Her eyes flashed tinges of red and orange. I could smell her desire.

I growled. I curled my lips, showing my sharp teeth. I would rip her skin apart if she touched one of my puppies. I stood tall. She

did not frighten me. She could never get past me. I would sink my teeth into her nasty smelly bottom so that she would never be able to sit down again.

NOTE: To hurt a human is the greatest crime a dog can commit. Yet for a human to hurt a dog is just as bad. This is the unspoken word between us.

"Those are puppies?" Cruella's lip curled in disgust. "They look like white rats."

"Their spots don't come until later," Anita explained.

"You're sure?"

"Yes."

Cruella nodded her head curtly. "All right. Put them in a bag. I'll take them with me now."

"They were just born," Roger protested.

"I can see that."

"Cruella, they have to be with their mother for several weeks," Anita told her. "They're not ready to leave."

"Fine. Then put them on reserve for me." She opened her purse and pulled out her checkbook and pen. "How much would you like?"

"They're not for sale," Roger said firmly.

"You've come into some money, have you?" Cruella said with withering scorn. "Did you design some silly game that will drive delinquent kiddies into a frenzy of video delight?"

"As a matter of fact . . ." Roger's voice was low and angry.

"We're not sure we're going to sell the puppies," Anita quickly interrupted. "That's what Roger meant to say."

"How many are there?" Cruella demanded.

Anita answered. "Fifteen."

"Fifteen times . . . five hundred pounds? Seventy-five hundred pounds," she concluded. "Fair? Two pounds per spot?" Cruella opened the checkbook and began making out the check.

"Why would you want fifteen puppies?" Anita asked.

"It's irrelevant, Anita," Roger said. "She can't have any. They're not for sale."

Cruella's eyes narrowed. "I'm getting very tired of you, Roland." She tore the check from the book and held it out to Anita. "Take it."

Anita looked at Roger for a clue as what to do. In her basket on the floor, Perdy whimpered with fear.

Cruella rattled the check. "Take it!" she ordered.

Anita took a breath. "Cruella, the puppies aren't for sale."

"You're quite sure?"

"Yes," she and Roger answered together.

Stunned, Cruella glared at them. Then she ripped the check into pieces and threw the pieces in Anita's face. "You're a fool," she said furiously. "I have no use for fools. You're fired. You're finished. You'll never work in fashion again. What a pity. Enjoy your poverty; revel in your obscurity."

As she stomped from the room, Cruella turned to Roger. Her eyes glittered with a cold malice. "Remember. I had her first."

The front door slammed behind her.

CHAPTER 9

Dognapping!

"I've got them! They're here!" Nanny came through the door, set a package wrapped in brown paper on a bureau, and took off her coat. A wave of puppies cascaded down the stairs and, yipping joyously, surrounded her.

"To the kitchen, everyone! Anita! Roger!"

Inside the package were fifteen small boxes. Anita opened the first one. "Jewel?" she said. A small puppy with spots in the shape of necklace stepped forward. Slowly Anita fastened a red-leather dog collar around her neck. On it was a brass tag engraved with her name.

"Dipstick?" Roger called.

Then it was Nanny's turn. "Fidget?"

"Two-Tone?"

Soon fourteen of the puppies were wearing new collars. Anita picked up the last collar and looked around for its owner. She heard a tinkle on the kitchen floor. A puppy peeked shame-facedly out from beneath the table.

"Wizzer," Anita and Roger sighed in unison.

"I'll get the mop," Nanny said.

From their truck, Jasper and Horace watched as Anita, Roger, Pongo, and Perdy set out on their evening walk. As soon as they were around the corner, the two thugs took off their caps, yanked black panty hose over their heads, and replaced the caps.

"Let's go," Jasper growled.

The two men reached for the doors; then Jasper leaned back and glared at Horace. They couldn't move—they had put the same pair of panty hose on their heads.

Every evening, Perdy and I put our humans on their leashes and take them for a walk. It is most practical when our little ones are asleep.

Nanny puppy-sits.

At the kitchen counter, Nanny cleaned up after the puppies, scooping the leftovers from their dishes. "Somebody didn't finish their supper," she grumbled. "We're on a budget. There's no accounting for waste."

The doorbell rang. Nanny went to the door and opened it a crack.

Two men with black panty hose over their faces stood on the step. They tipped their caps to her. "Evening, ma'am."

With a shriek, Nanny flung herself against the door, but Jasper quickly wedged his foot in.

Horace leaned forward. "It's all right, lady," he said loudly. "We're professionals!" He winced as Jasper elbowed him in the side to shut him up.

Frantically Nanny tried to hold the door closed and screamed loudly, hoping someone, anyone, would hear. Suddenly, the security chain tore loose. The two men pushed their way into the house.

From the closet underneath the stairs came Nanny's muffled screams. Jasper and Horace peeled off their panty hose masks and made their way to the kitchen.

"The old bird put up a good fight," Jasper said. "I admire spirit in a gal."

"Easy for you to say," Horace grumbled. "You didn't take a boot in the backside." He took the burlap sack that Jasper held out to him.

"Hold the bag. I'll get the puppies." Jasper ripped open the curtains under the sink. The puppies huddled behind Wizzer, who growled fearlessly, then lunged and clamped his teeth on Jasper's finger.

Meanwhile Horace had spotted an uncovered dish of leftover dog food. He sniffed it, smiled, and picked up a spoon.

"The bag!" Jasper shrieked. Pain did not improve his temper.

Putting the food aside, Horace held the bag open while Jasper tossed the puppies into it. "That's the lot," Jasper snarled. "Let's get out of here."

Horace took another bite of dog food. "Mmmm. Good."

"What is the matter with you?" asked Jasper.

"I haven't eaten since breakfast." Horace held out a spoonful to Jasper, who recoiled in disgust.

"What do you think this is?" he demanded.

Horace chewed thoughtfully. "I don't have to think. I know. It's pâté." He scooped out the last bit and set the empty container aside. "A nice duck pâté with pistachio nuts and fennel."

"You're a bloody stupid jerk," Jasper jeered. "You're eating dog food." With a loud laugh, he swung the bag of puppies over his back and walked

out of the house.

Flushed with pride, Jasper strolled down the street with the bag of whimpering puppies slung over his back.

"Evening, general." He tipped his head to an older man walking a bulldog along the street.

The bulldog turned and barked ferociously at Jasper. His owner tugged on his leash.

"Montgomery! Heel, boy!"

Jasper ignored the dog. He opened the back of his truck and tossed the sack of puppies in.

"You know what I think, Jasper?

"Horace glanced fearfully at the barking dog. "I think that bulldog knows what we just done."

"Dogs ain't got the mind to figure things out, Horace. Chances are the mutt's just got a whiff of the horse meat on your breath." He locked the truck and put his hand reassuringly on his partner's shoulder. "The downfall of the canine population is that they're too stupid to realize that there's some among us what want to do them harm."

**W**e were strolling along, enjoying our evening walk. Perdy and I were discussing Wizzer's little problem, when the tranquillity of the evening—and our lives–was shattered with three sharp barks . . .

WOOF! WOOF! WOOF!

The K-911 emergency bark.

Something was terribly wrong. Perdy and I pulled our leashes free from Roger and Anita and ran home.

We rushed into the house.

The puppies were gone!

A trace of secondhand perfume hung in the air. I sniffed the basket and all around for clues.

SNIFF. SNIFF. SNIFF. SNUFFLE.

Meat-eating thieves. Two of them. Each odor similar in nature, but distinctly different. Dirty, stinking, disgusting, and greedy! Leather boots. Greasy hair. Bad tempered and mean.

Wizzer is so brave, I'm sure he bit the thieves. And with any luck Two-Tone did his stuff! I hope they are being brave.

C H A P T E R   1 0

Animal Rally

When the phone rang, Cruella was lying on a sofa in her library and smoking a cigarette. Across from her, a visitor sat by the fire.

"Evening, ma'am." said Jasper on the other end of the line. "I sincerely hope I'm not disturbing your relaxation but I've got good news."

"Did you get the puppies?" At his answer, her face brightened. "All of them?" She took a long drag on her cigarette. "My faith in your limited intelligence is momentarily restored."

"You're too kind, ma'am."

Cruella hung up the phone. "They've got the fifteen," she said to her visitor. "Anita's finally paid me back for all I've done for her. Poor thing, she'll never know how much it means to me." Her cold laughter echoed through the room.

Lionel Skinner took out a notebook and pen from his pocket and began to calculate. He added the fifteen to another number and wrote down the total: ninety-nine.

In the back of the truck, Wizzer wriggled and squirmed until he had forced an opening in the bag that imprisoned him and his brothers and sisters. Then he squeezed through and sniffed at the rust hole in the back door. Was anyone out there? He gave a short, sharp bark.

A terrier named Kipper, lying in the doorway of a nearby cottage, pricked up his ears. He stumbled to his feet and barked a response.

Making their way toward the truck, Jasper and Horace stumbled out of the pub. "I'm gonna go to bed," Jasper yawned. "I'm dead tired."

Horace cocked his head. "I'm hearing dogs again, Jasper."

Jasper drew his leg back and kicked the rusting door of the truck. "Shut up in there!" he bawled. He got into the cab and started up the truck.

Kipper ran after it, as fast as his short legs could carry him. But at the top of a hill he stopped, panting and exhausted. The truck rumbled away and was lost in the dark, moonlit night.

The fire in Roger and Anita's living room crackled. But Pongo and Perdy were listless and mournful and deeply worried about the fate of their puppies. They weren't comforted by the warmth of the fire.

"They're going to do their best." Nanny had just spoken to the police.

Roger shook his head. "For what that's worth."

"Do you think they'll find them?" Anita asked anxiously.

"I have my doubts they'll even look," Roger sighed. "In a city of ten million people, fifteen lost puppies don't mean much."

 must find them! I will alert the neighborhood and send the word across England!

K-911.

THE SIGNAL THAT IS NEVER SENT UNLESS THE NEED IS DESPERATE (AND NO DOG EVER FAILS TO RESPOND).

HELP! HELP! HELP! WOOF! WOOF! WOOF!

FIFTEEN DALMATIAN PUPPIES STOLEN . . . SEND NEWS TO PONGO AND PERDY OF REGENT'S PARK, LONDON.

END OF MESSAGE.

Downstairs, Perdy lifted her head at the sound of Pongo's barking. She rose and trotted quietly up the stairs.

In the master bedroom, Roger jumped out of bed. "Pongo's on the roof!" he cried, dashing toward the stairway. Grabbing a bathrobe, Anita scrambled after him.

"It won't do any good to wake up the neighborhood," Roger said to Pongo as he led him across the roof by the collar.

Anita had hold of Perdy. "We know how you feel," she said sympathetically, "but that won't bring your puppies back."

Pongo's barking had already done its work. From Buckingham Palace to the London streets, corgis, Scotties, mutts, and mongrels passed the signal to one another. Pongo's message traveled out of the city and into the country.

On a rocky hilltop, a Border collie listened to the message. His answering bark echoed through the woods.

In a nearby barn, a draft horse named Punch hung his head out the window and listened attentively. Next to him, an old English sheepdog snored on his back in the hay.

Punch turned away from the window and whinnied loudly. Fogey, the sheepdog, awoke with a jolt. Barking madly, he jumped to his feet and charged into the aisle. Punch swung his head toward the window and snorted.

Fogey galloped to the window. As the Border collie barked out the message once more, Fogey repeated it, trying to get it exactly right. Punch took up the signal by slamming his hoof over and over on the wooden floor.

In response, cows mooed, pigs oinked, chickens clucked, and sheep rose from sleep and headed down a field. And Kipper, the dog who had talked to Wizzer, streaked across the hills, toward the sound of Fogey's bark.

When Kipper ran through the barn door, all the animals were gathered in a circle around Fogey. Kipper pantomimed what he knew: he snagged an empty feed sack and, whimpering like the Dalmatian puppies, wiggled into it; then he walked out of the barn on his hind legs, with the bag in his mouth.

The animals cawed, woofed, whinnied, mooed, and oinked to let him know they understood. Then Kipper led Fogey to the top of a nearby hill and struck a pointer's stance. Fogey peered into the night. There was the abandoned De Vil mansion a few miles away—but its lights were on and smoke curled darkly from its chimney. The two dogs exchanged glances. With a short bark, Kipper took off toward the mansion to find the puppies.

Fogey galloped back to the farmyard and barked out a message, using a discarded piece of a farm building as a megaphone. On a nearby hilltop, the collie took up the message:

"CALLING PONGO AND PERDY OF REGENT'S PARK, LONDON . . . THE NEWS IS GOOD. YOUR PUPPIES ARE SAFE. THEY ARE SIXTY MILES WEST OF LONDON AND FOUR HUNDRED AND EIGHTY-TWO DOGS AWAY. I HEARD IT FROM A CORGI, WHO HEARD IT FROM A SHEEPDOG, WHO HEARD IT FROM A PEKINGESE, WHO HEARD IT FROM A TERRIER, WHO HEARD IT FROM A DOBERMAN. HURRY—WE WILL GUIDE YOU."

CHAPTER 11

Prime Suspect

Cruella's morning newspaper blared the news: DOGNAPPING! accompanied by a picture of Nanny sitting by the empty puppy basket.

"Dognapping," she sneered. "Can you imagine?"

Another paper lying on her bed had a different caption: FIFTEEN PUPPIES STOLEN. THIEVES FLEE.

"Fifteen puppies stolen. What precious little creatures." Cruella's voice dripped venom. "Anita and her fool."

She glanced at a picture of Roger and Anita. "Such sad faces. Such sorrow." Cruella laughed. Then she picked up her phone.

The ringing woke Anita and Roger from a sound sleep. "It's Scotland Yard!" Roger grabbed the receiver. "Hello, Inspector?"

He paused. "Who?"

Anita leaned forward anxiously. "What are they saying? Have they found them?"

Roger shook his head and handed her the phone.

"Hello?" For a moment, Anita didn't recognize the voice at the other end, and when she did, she wasn't glad to hear it. "Cruella?"

"Anita, darling." Lying back against the pillows of her bed, Cruella smiled, then continued smoothly. "I saw the papers. It's a dreadful thing. You must be crushed." She took a long drag from her cigarette. "I know that

our parting was unpleasant and that my words were harsh, but at a time like this, our differences don't matter. Do they?"

Anita felt herself softening. "I don't suppose so."

"Is she calling to confess?" Roger demanded.

Anita covered the phone and shot him an indignant look. "Roger, please!"

Don't listen to her," he pleaded.

"Yes," Anita said to Cruella, "we're doing everything we can."

"I spoke with the police. And Scotland Yard. I'm very sorry to say that I wasn't much help. Have they offered any information?"

Anita was silent.

Roger grabbed the phone from Anita. "Where are they?!" he yelled into the receiver.

Anita snatched the phone back from her husband. "What's the matter with you?" she cried.

"Anita?" Cruella's voice came from the dangling receiver.

"I'm sorry, Cruella," Anita apologized. "He's very upset. If there's any news, I'll let you know. Thanks for calling."

She hung up and turned to Roger. "That was uncalled for. She may be a lot of things but she's not a thief."

"For me, she's the prime suspect."

"She's been investigated by Scotland Yard. What more do you want?"

Roger shook his head and sighed. "I don't know. I'm sorry. I just feel so helpless."

"However helpless we feel, just imagine how Pongo and Perdy feel."

While Anita and Roger were talking, a Chihuahua trotted around the corner, sat down in front of their house, and began to bark.

Inside the house, Perdy nudged Pongo awake. The two dogs scrambled to their feet and barked excitedly.

The Chihuahua howled in response. The two dogs charged for the door. With a quick, practiced motion, Pongo unlatched it and they ran out.

"Pongo!" Roger heard the familiar sound of the door unlatching. "He opened the door!" He rushed to the window, while Anita hurried after him. "Pongo!" he shouted. "Perdy!"

With stunned looks on their faces, Roger and Anita watched their dogs disappear down the street.

ur journey began. It didn't take long to leave the city lights and enter the moonlit fields. The night was cold. The water troughs were iced over, and the wind was bitter. Perdy and I were guided by the twilight barking. We spoke very little. Our messages came to us across the frosty fields loud and clear.

Skinner was at his bench, tanning a hide, when the ancient black phone on his desk began to ring.

"Mr. Skinner?" The voice of Cruella De Vil came over the line. "How are you?" She paused for a moment, not expecting him to answer. "Suspicions are mounting," she said. "It's time."

Skinner smiled and ran his thumb across the blade of a knife.

"Will you be able to do it tonight?" Cruella demanded.

He tapped his yellow-stained finger once on the mouthpiece.

"All of it?"

He tapped again.

"You'll get paid when you deliver the fur." Cruella paused. Her voice turned cold. "Enjoy."

CHAPTER 12

Kipper to the Rescue

At the De Vil mansion, Horace and Jasper sat on old ripped chairs in front of a dying fire. "Stand up a minute there, mate," Jasper said. "Fire's getting a bit dim."

Horace stood up. Quickly Jasper pulled the chair out from behind him, tossed it into the fire, and then returned to his own seat.

The chair burst into flames. Without noticing, Horace lowered himself down and crashed to the floor.

Kipper leaped onto a balcony rail, sailed through a broken window in the De Vil mansion, and fell through the rotted cloth of a bed canopy. An enormous cloud of dust billowed around him as he landed on the ancient mattress. He jumped down to the floor and sniffed his way down the hall.

"I'll be honest with you, mate." Horace sat on the sagging sofa and untied his shoes. "This job is losing its charm. The housing stinks, the food's lousy, the lavatory facilities are appalling, and, so far, we ain't been paid so much as a quid."

Jasper sprawled on the other side, trying to avoid the protruding sofa springs. "Aw, quit your crying. It's all over tomorrow night. We gets our boodle and we'll be gone fast as you can say 'dead puppies.'"

Horace bent over to take off his shoes. Was there something moving in the shadows? "Jasper? Did we make sure them puppies was locked up?"

"We counted every bloody one of them," Jasper said with a belch.

The room was a mess—like the rest of the mansion. There was broken furniture, splintering walls, rotting carpets, and crumbling ceilings. Kipper made his way to a set of closed doors and scratched at them. He smelled the puppies somewhere nearby.

From the other side of the door came a little cry. They were there! Kipper looked anxiously around for a way to get to them. With a tiny squeak, a mouse scampered in front of him. Using its tail as a pointer, it showed Kipper the bent grill of a heating vent. Kipper wagged his tail and squeezed through.

He emerged from behind the arm of a torn, filthy sofa in the library. There were Dalmatian puppies everywhere: on chairs, bookshelves, tables, and windowsills; under sofas; behind curtains; and in the corners. There were ninety-nine puppies altogether!

With Kipper leading them, the puppies crept through the grill and out of the library. As the last one emerged, Kipper stepped around the corner. Suddenly Horace lumbered out of the drawing room and stood in the hallway, listening carefully. Kipper and the puppies shrank back into the shadows.

With a suspicious scowl on his face, Horace scanned the lounge and checked the library doors. Then he headed to the bathroom.

The line of puppies continued silently toward the entry. All went well until one of the smallest puppies stumbled and slid into a table. A crystal lamp teetered and then crashed to the floor.

"Horace?" Jasper called.

The puppies raced back across the lounge and wriggled through the broken heating vent back into the library.

"Horace?" Jasper crossed to the steps and yanked a wooden railing from the rotting staircase. Brandishing it over his head, he marched to the library and threw the doors open.

No one was there—except the puppies, of course.

Horace flipped his magazine to the floor and headed toward the drawing room. He must have been imagining those noises.

Upstairs, Jasper heard the thud of the magazine. As he stopped to listen, a floorboard creaked under his foot.

When he heard the creak of the board, Horace grabbed a wooden railing and took a step forward. His eyes widened with fear as Jasper's shadow appeared on the wall, and he raised his weapon.

Suddenly the two men leaped into the doorway at the same time, screamed loudly, and whacked each other over the head.

e traveled through the frozen night. The darkness was our place of hiding. We were silent. We were sad.

Without warning, and without permission, a particularly large and heavy bird landed on my nose and pecked me on the head! Now, I am quite aware that birds do not possess the best of manners, as they are commonly known to drop droppings carelessly from the sky without looking to see what or who is below! But I had never before encountered such rudeness as this! I was just about to snap at the little feathered rascal when he began chirping in my ear.

"HIGH-VOLTAGE ELECTRIC FENCE AHEAD. FOLLOW ME. I KNOW OF A SECRET SPACE. SORRY IF I SCARED YOU."

I thanked our feathered friend and we followed him to a gap in the fence that was just large enough for us to squeeze through.

Perdy's feet were sore and bleeding. We were both tired. We had not eaten, and even when morning came, the chill of the night remained.

His temper none the better for the blow on the head, Horace entered the library. The puppies cowered before him. One looked especially forlorn.

"You're hungry, ain'tcha?" Horace grinned maliciously. "I brung you something to eat."

He pulled out a mousetrap with a piece of cheese resting in the trip plate. With a mean laugh, he set the trap on the floor.

"What're you doing?" Jasper demanded, coming into the room. "I asked you to check on the mutts. Not keep 'em company."

Horace pointed to the trap. "Look."

The puppy sniffed the cheese. Jasper scowled, grabbed Horace by the arm, and shoved him out the door.

"It was only a joke," Horace whined as Jasper kicked the door shut.

"It's a waste of cheese," Jasper retorted and pushed Horace ahead.

"Not to worry. It's a bit old and smelly."

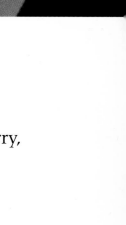

"Pongo and Perdy will turn up," Anita said forlornly to Roger. "Won't they?"

Roger stared at the fire. He didn't know what to say.

"If you ask me, they will." Nanny carried a tray of tea things into the living room. "They just went looking for the puppies."

"They won't find them, Nanny," Anita said. "I know they're gone."

"You can't lose hope, dear," Nanny said gently.

"You know who did this, don't you?" Roger said harshly.

"I know what you're thinking," Anita said. "And you're wrong."

"I don't think so." Roger reached for his tea.

"I, for one, wouldn't be the least surprised," Nanny said. "I'm sorry, dear," she apologized to Anita, "but I wouldn't put it past her. She has an awful temper."

Anita looked troubled.

"The dogs never cared for her." Nanny sat down in a chair.

"Roger!" Anita jumped to her feet. "Where's my portfolio?"

A few minutes later, she was kneeling on the nursery floor, throwing aside large sheets of drawing paper. Suddenly the color drained from her face. She looked up. "Oh no. You're right. Cruella stole the puppies. This is why."

Tears streamed down Anita's face as she handed the drawing to Roger. It was the picture of the black spotted coat she had designed for Cruella. "She's going to kill the puppies!" Anita cried.

Gleaming knives lay against black satin. Lionel Skinner snapped the case shut and loaded his equipment into the old hearse he used as a car. Everything was there: spanners, stretchers, chemicals, tools. He slammed the back door shut and climbed behind the wheel.

Anita and Roger stood at the door of Cruella's city residence. "Can you tell me where she's gone?" Roger asked.

"I would like to oblige you, sir," the butler answered, "but I'm not at liberty to divulge madam's whereabouts."

Anita stepped forward. "Cruella knows me. I worked for her. I'm a designer."

"Many people have worked for the firm," the butler said.

"She's going to do something

terrible!" Anita cried in desperation. "Can't you help us?"

The butler stared coldly at them. "I'm very sorry. Good evening."

"Will you give her a message?" Roger asked. "Tell her . . ."

The butler shut the door in his face.

". . . tell her we know all about her!" Roger yelled. "We're going to the police!"

CHAPTER 13

A Narrow Escape

At the De Vil mansion, the animals were busy. One squirrel gnawed on a wire in Horace and Jasper's truck, another poked its head out of a heating vent, while a third rolled a walnut into the tailpipe.

A few miles away, Pongo and Perdy slowed to a stop, uncertain of which way to go. A Border collie barked out a direction. They took off after him.

Jasper stretched and groaned. "I think it's time to let the little yappers have it."

"We ain't supposed to do it," Horace whined. "That's Skinner's job."

"Why should that little runt have all the fun?"

Horace grinned. "Howdja wanna do it?"

Crossing over to the fireplace, Jasper picked up a poker. "I personally favor the fire iron.

Horace kicked over a table and tore off one of its legs.

Just then, someone knocked at the door. The two men exchanged puzzled looks. "Must be the missus," Jasper said. "Fix your shirt and your hair."

Jasper and Horace smiled broadly, then swung the door open. Their smiles faded. "Hello? Anyone there?" Jasper called.

Behind him, Kipper led the puppies out of the library once again. They slipped around the corner and started up the stairs. Wizzer was the last in line. But neither he nor Kipper had noticed one more puppy, sound asleep behind the library door.

The two thugs slammed the front door. The knocking began again. They whipped it open. No one was there. Jasper and Horace stepped out on the porch, shining their flashlights into the bushes.

As the puppies made their escape, a woodpecker quietly flew away into the snowy night.

Kipper kept his eye on the line of puppies hurrying up the stairs. Just a few more . . .

The front door banged shut. "Maybe we was hearing things," Horace said loudly in the entryway.

Kipper's heart pounded. If they came in now, all hope was gone.

Just then, the truck horn honked loudly. Horace and Jasper ran outside. Three raccoons were sitting in the front seat.

"Get outta there!" Jasper screamed.

The raccoons hurried away, their job done. They had given the puppies a few more minutes of precious escape time.

As Wizzer rounded the corner, he saw the magazine that Horace had dropped. Cruella's picture was on the front cover. It was too tempting. Wizzer lifted his leg over the picture of Cruella. . . .

Then the front door slammed. "I don't believe me eyes!" Jasper's flashlight picked out Wizzer scrambling up the stairs, and then the puppies gathered on the landing above. Suddenly Kipper dashed down, grabbed Wizzer by the scruff of the neck, and charged up the stairs with him.

The two thugs ran after them. "Drop that puppy, you lousy . . ."

Just then they hit Wizzer's wet patch, skidded over the magazine, and crashed to the floor.

The puppies stampeded through the upstairs hallway.

Horace and Jasper rose slowly to their feet and marched up the stairs.

"I don't care what you say, I think we better bloody well be careful," Horace growled.

"You're afraid of puppies now?" Jasper sneered.

"It ain't about being afraid. It's about being careful."

"Careful of what?" Jasper said scornfully.

At that moment, their feet hit a missing tread on the staircase. The carpet runner yanked forward and, as they watched in horror, pulled a large cabinet toward the edge of the staircase. It stopped and swayed threateningly above them.

Suddenly Horace and Jasper

crashed through the stairs. The cabinet's upper doors swung open, spilling a hundred paperweights down on them.

In a crockery closet beneath the stairs, Horace and Jasper stood waist-deep in broken jars and paperweights. "Bloody good thing that cabinet didn't fall on us," Horace muttered.

The cabinet teetered delicately on the edge of the stairs. Wizzer gave it a small push with his nose and it toppled forward, crashed onto the stairs, and slid halfway down, covering the gaping hole that Horace and Jasper had made. The two men turned on their flashlights just as the lower doors burst open, dumping forks, spoons, and knives over their heads.

As the puppies made their way to the top of the mansion, Jasper and Horace fought their way out of the basement.

Kipper nosed open a service door and led the puppies onto the roof. Peering over the edge, he saw Fogey down below in the service court and barked out a greeting. One of the puppies slid down the roof and landed in the broad gutter below. One by one, the others followed him. But Wizzer turned and went back into the house. He had something to do before he left.

"It's your great bulk that caused that last calamity," Jasper snarled at Horace.

Horace scowled. "I ain't taking any more lip from you."

"Quit your whining." Jasper shoved him hard. "We have ninety-nine stinking dogs to find and kill. Get to it."

Wizzer sat very still in the hallway. A slow grin spread across Jasper's face when he saw him. "Come here, you speckled lap rat," he crooned nastily.

The puppy didn't move. Jasper raced toward him, and when he saw the hole, it was too late to stop. He fell straight down and landed on a billiard table, which collapsed under his weight.

Jasper stared into the face of a stuffed water buffalo directly above him. With a creak, it dropped on top of him, pinning him to the table.

Horace ran through a bedroom, narrowly missed the hole that Jasper had just fallen through, and flashed his light up and down the hallway. There was Wizzer, racing for the linens room. Horace rushed after him. He'd get that puppy now. It couldn't escape.

But the room was empty. There was nothing but snow, ice, tar stains, and a gaping broken wall with a long drop to the ground.

"Where've you gone to, you little bugger?" Horace cursed.

Wizzer forced himself to lie silently on his belly, so he would blend in with the snow and the tar stains. The flashlight passed over him; Horace did not see him.

One by one, the puppies slid down the copper spout and rolled into the snow, where Fogey shepherded them into the deep woods. On the mansion roof, Kipper placed the last puppy in the gutter. He looked around, then barked. Wizzer was missing. Kipper charged across the roof to the stairs.

Wizzer looked out the hole in the wall. It was a very long drop to the ground from here and it didn't look like a soft landing. Below him was

the hard, frozen ice of a duck pond. Wizzer turned and looked in the other direction. There was Horace and his flashlight.

Suddenly, Kipper appeared in the doorway. He growled angrily at Wizzer and motioned him up the attic stairwell.

Wizzer trotted across to him. But he couldn't resist one last fierce bark at Horace's retreating back.

Horace spun around and trained his flashlight in the direction of the bark. The beam lit up Wizzer's little tail wagging defiantly at the bottom of the staircase.

In a rage, Horace rushed after him. He hit the ice on the linen-room floor, skidded across the room, and sailed out the hole in the wall.

Wizzer barked triumphantly, then charged up the stairs.

Down below, a beam of light flashed wildly across the duck pond, followed by a long scream. Horace crashed through the ice and sank to the bottom of the pond.

Reunited

Feeling very pleased with herself, Cruella drove through the deep snow of the countryside in her Panther De Vil. She was driving recklessly but she didn't care. Danger exhilarated her. She blasted her horn and sped through a village. The moment she had been waiting for had almost arrived.

Kipper watched Wizzer slide down the copper pipe to safety. With a sigh of relief, he turned toward the roof door.

There stood a battered, dusty, bruised Jasper, with a fireplace poker held high over his head. "It's time to pay the piper," he snarled.

Kipper dodged as Jasper swung at him again and again. Suddenly he lunged and clamped his teeth on Jasper's hand.

With a howl, Jasper dropped the poker. Kipper bared his teeth and growled fiercely.

Jasper pushed his coat aside and yanked out his pistol. "I'm very sorry," he hissed, "but I'm going to have to bid you adieu."

Terrified, Kipper backed to the edge of the roof. His back paws scraped against the tar, then slipped. He hung by his front paws for a moment, then fell to the ground.

Jasper looked down at Kipper's limp body and laughed. "Stupid mutt . . . ," he scratched his head with the barrel of his pistol,

". . . gun ain't even loaded."

The pistol discharged, blowing Jasper's hat and toupee off his head.

Just then, Cruella's Panther De Vil came to a screeching halt in front of the mansion. Jasper froze in panic. "The missus! Horace!" he bawled.

As Cruella stepped out of her car, he saluted her from the roof. "Evening, ma'am," he said smoothly.

Cruella looked up angrily. "What are you doing up there?!" As she impatiently tapped her left foot, a skunk waddled out of the bushes and wiggled into the driver's seat of her car—positioning himself right next to her black-and-white fur purse.

Jasper was silent.

"Answer me!" she shrieked.

"I was fetching the puppies, ma'am," he stuttered in terror.

Cruella's eyes narrowed. "And where are the puppies?" she demanded furiously.

Jasper shifted from one foot to the other. "I'm not entirely certain. I'd have to check with my associate. Horace?"

A few yards away, a frozen Horace tried to crawl out of the pond. He was covered in ice from the tip of his nose to his feet.

Jasper cupped his hands around his mouth. "Horace!"

With a crunch of breaking ice, Horace stood up.

Cruella shook her fist at Jasper. "Get down from there and catch those puppies!" There was a threat in her voice, which she meant to carry out if she didn't see those puppies soon.

Meanwhile, the policemen came out of Cruella De Vil's London residence carrying the pelt of the slaughtered tiger from the London Zoo.

On the sidewalk, Anita turned pale. Roger put a protective arm around her.

"Your suspicions were justified," the captain said, gesturing to the skin. "According to the staff, Ms. De Vil left early in the day for family property in Suffolk. Officers will be on the lookout for your puppies and Ms. De Vil." He paused, then said grimly, "I hope we're not too late."

Fogey watched over his flock, resting in the deep snow that covered the sheep meadow.

A short distance away, Cruella's Panther De Vil pulled up by the side of the road. She gazed suspiciously at the puppy tracks that seemed to lead straight to the sheep. Something was wrong here. Still, there was no sign of the puppies. Cruella rolled up her window and drove the car away.

As the car drove out of sight, the sheep rose to their feet. Ninety-eight puppies tumbled out from beneath them. Fogey barked an order and they continued on their trek.

At the De Vil mansion, a trembling-cold Horace, encrusted with icicles, climbed into the truck.

"You just had to let them puppies slip away, didn't you?" said a furious Jasper. "Never paying attention!"

"Where was you?" Horace sulked.

"I wasn't splashing about in a pond! If we don't get them puppies back, it's quite literally our heads."

He turned the key over and over in the starter. The engine sputtered feebly. "Go out and check the tailpipe," he ordered. "I think we got a condensation problem."

"One of these days, I'm gonna be full up of you!" Horace muttered. He waddled to the back of the truck. "What's it I'm looking for?"

"Moisture in the tailpipe!" Jasper screamed.

With a sullen nod, Horace crouched in front of the tailpipe. Jasper floored the gas pedal. The engine fired. The walnut that the squirrel had shoved in the tailpipe exploded out like a shot and blasted Horace.

At the farmstead, the crow greeted a weary and cold Perdy and Pongo with a loud caw. The horse Punch poked his head out and whinnied a welcome. The two dogs squeezed in through a hole in the side of the barn and rushed down the aisle, looking for their puppies.

Eventually, we reached a shabby old farm.

A cow mooed.

MOOOOOOOOOO!!!!

Obediently, we followed her call.

Perdy's head disappeared into a hole in the cow's stall.

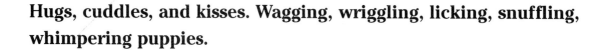

I held my breath and crossed my paws. Her tail began to wag furiously, and little yapping noises seemed to burst from everywhere!

Oh, I had missed them so very much!

Hugs, cuddles, and kisses. Wagging, wriggling, licking, snuffling, whimpering puppies.

ONE . . . TWO . . . THREE . . . FOUR . . . FIVE . . . SIX . . . SEVEN . . . EIGHT . . . NINE . . . TEN . . . ELEVEN . . . TWELVE . . . THIRTEEN . . . FOURTEEN . . . FIFTEEN . . . SIXTEEN . . . SEVENTEEN . . . WHAT? EIGHTEEN . . . TWENTY-SEVEN . . . FORTY-NINE . . . SEVENTY . . . NINETY-EIGHT!!!!

NINETY-EIGHT PUPPIES . . . all in big trouble, yet howling with delight! I looked at Perdy. She nodded her head, and with her tired eyes, she said to me, "Of course, we can keep them, too, and love them as our own."

Back at the mansion, one small puppy whimpered sadly. He had been asleep when the others left. Now he was alone and lost and afraid. He wondered if he would ever find them.

Cruella leaned out of her car and gazed at a set of tracks leading to the farmstead. She smiled and took a drag on her cigarette. The puppies were nearby. This time they wouldn't get away.

Carelessly she flicked her ash on the passenger seat. The skunk looked up indignantly.

Pongo and Fogey peered out of a hole in the barn wall. Fogey grumbled. Something was wrong; he could smell the danger in the air.

Outside the barn where the Dalmatians hid, Cruella's car rolled to a silent stop.

Fogey barked an alert, and Pongo and Perdy scrambled out from the stalls, with the puppies following.

I tried to impress upon the ninety-eight wiggling puppies that this escape required tremendous organization:

We will form a line, noses to tails, and quickly march straight out of here without being seen.

1. No tail wagging—too noisy.
2. No yapping.
3. No whining.
4. No whimpering.
5. No playing.
6. No stopping.
7. No scratching.
8. No licking.
9. No chatting.

"**T**his is extraordinary," Cruella spat out as she picked her way through the mud. "I have to tramp through the mud and muck because those morons can't keep track of a bunch of infant dogs."

At the sound of her voice, Pongo and Perdy herded the puppies down the aisle. Punch stood ready to defend the doors.

Cruella stopped, pulled out a tissue, and wiped a spot of mud from her shoe. As she straightened up, the crow sailed out of the barn window, swooped over her head, and snatched her fur hat.

Cruella screamed and stamped her feet. "Jasper! Horace!" Where were those fools when she needed them?

Jasper and Horace's truck lurched along the road. The lights flashed on and off while Jasper pounded the wheel in a fury.

"Turn on the heat, will ya?" Horace hadn't been able to warm up since falling into the frozen pond.

"Not with this thing acting like it is. I don't want to risk losing power."

"Well, I can't stand the cold no more! I want heat!" Horace flipped a switch. Flames shot out from the heating vents. The men screamed as the cab turned into an inferno. The truck swerved into a snowbank, its doors flew open, and the two men leaped out.

Their faces black with soot, Jasper and Horace picked themselves up.

"We bloody well better have that heater adjusted," Horace grumbled.

Jasper shot him a menacing look. "What did I say about the heat? What did I SAY?"

"I don't want you yelling at me right now," Horace muttered.

"Because you know you done wrong?" his partner demanded.

"No."

"Because you know you're the stupidest toe rag the European Community's ever gonna produce?"

"No," Horace said stubbornly.

Jasper grabbed him by the throat. "Then tell me why you don't think I oughta yell at you right now?"

"We ain't got the time."

"Oh? Why not?"

"Because the truck's gonna blow up."

An ominous hissing came from the truck. The two men looked at each other, then hurled themselves off the road as the truck exploded in a ball of fire.

Cruella peered through a knothole in the barn doors. There was nothing to see but the back of a horse.

Suddenly the horse whinnied and his hooves slammed into the doors. They burst open, sending Cruella flying across the yard and into the muck.

Horace and Jasper rose to their knees to survey the damage. Their truck was a wreck. Nothing was left but a twisted frame and burning tires.

"My truck's gone," Jasper whimpered in shock. "Reduced to a burning hulk."

"When are you going to listen to me?" Horace whined. "It's the animals! They done this to us."

"I don't want to hear no more of that twaddle!" Jasper snarled. "If this is the work of dumb animals, then I'll clasp me hands together, turn me eyes to the heavens, and beg that I'm struck senseless by our dear . . ."

His voice died out. Hurtling down from the skies, straight at his head, was the grill of the truck. Thinking quickly, Jasper grabbed Horace and thrust him directly underneath it.

CHAPTER 15

All 101

Lionel Skinner walked slowly up the broken steps of the De Vil mansion. As he entered, he bowed and tipped his hat to the puppy in a mock greeting.

The puppy who had been left behind greeted him with a happy yip. Then he realized his mistake. This man had not come to rescue him. In terror, the pup backed away.

With a gloved hand, Skinner reached for him.

Suddenly Skinner heard a growl behind him. A bruised and battered Kipper limped forward, his teeth bared menacingly.

As Skinner stared, the dog charged. Skinner opened his mouth in a silent scream as Kipper's jaws closed around his ankle.

Kipper charged again. Skinner fell to the floor, clutching both ankles in agony.

With the puppy in tow, Kipper hobbled to the door.

Puppies streamed silently out the hole in the side of the barn as Cruella walked through the barn doors. "Now listen to me, you country bumpkins—you obviously have no idea what you are mucking about with. You know what I'm here for. The puppies! If you don't want to hand them over to me immediately, I will simply rip your sorry heads from your bodies and personally sauté, soufflé, skewer, and skin your squealing carcasses into shish kebabs and hand luggage!"

A flock of chickens had gathered on the crossbeam above her.

Cruella smiled and looked up. The puppies, at last, she thought.

Instead, a shower of eggs dropped from the rafters, drenching her clothes and dribbling down her face and shoulders.

Cruella cleared her throat. She would give them one more chance. "I have an announcement to make."

A final egg plopped on her head.

Cruella was losing patience. She rammed a pitchfork into a pile of straw. "I know you're in here!" she said furiously.

A wagging tail in the hayloft just above caught her eye. Setting the pitchfork aside, she reached up with both hands and yanked. "I got you!" she cried.

A plump pink pig toppled over and pinned Cruella to the floor of the barn.

Horace and Jasper dragged a log over to an electric fence. "You don't got natural wits," Jasper scolded him. "That's your problem. You would have grabbed hold of that fence, given yourself a nasty jolt, and cooked your tongue before ever thinking it was electrified."

He spit on the wire. It sizzled and popped.

"Point well taken," Horace said, "but what's the log for?"

Jasper spoke slowly and distinctly. "We stand upon it and hop over the fence, avoiding painful, electric shock."

"Sounds like a plan," Horace agreed.

The two men stepped onto the log. "Raise the leg," Jasper ordered. "Swing 'er out. And push off with the other."

They bent their knees. Horace began to tip and lean away from the fence. Jasper leaned with him.

"Careful!" Horace cried.

"Look out!" Jasper yelled. The log rolled toward the fence. "Jump!"

The log rolled under the bottom wire, and Jasper and Horace were left only halfway over the electric fence. Horace wobbled wildly, then fell on his bottom. Wires buzzed; sparks flew. Blue electricity lit up crazily around him.

Jasper's mouth flew open and his hat and toupee exploded off.

The two men vaulted into the air, then landed heavily in the snow, their limbs vibrating with an electrical charge. They were still crackling and buzzing with electricity as they got up and disappeared into the woods.

"Useless, disgusting animals," Cruella snarled. She climbed to the hayloft. She wouldn't give up; no, never. But what was that in the distance? A line of Dalmatians, heading for town.

We will walk a few miles a day. The older pups will carry the younger ones when they get tired. I will send a barking message ahead of us for our friends to save us a little food and water in each village. The journey is long, but we must keep moving, as the thieves will be looking for us.

They had gotten away. In spite of her best efforts, they had escaped. She stumbled toward the stairs, then stopped suddenly. A raccoon was holding her fur hat. "Darling, red is not your color," she said. As she made her way toward the animal, two other raccoons released a trapdoor. Cruella fell through the open floor to the cellar. "Whoa!" She landed in a vat of thick, gooey molasses and, with a giant sucking sound, disappeared under the surface. A few seconds later, she emerged, glazed with molasses and sticking to the side of the vat as she tried to climb out.

When she finally stood up, molasses stretched like wires in long, rubbery strands from her body to the vat.

Still twitching and shaking, Horace and Jasper emerged from the woods. "Thank heavens!" Jasper cried fervently.

"We're saved!" Horace echoed.

Police cars and a paddy wagon lined the road. As Jasper and Horace were escorted inside, they smiled happily.

"This looks lovely," said Horace.

"Nice and warm," Jasper agreed.

"No animals, neither," Horace pronounced.

They sat down on the bench seat.

"Thanks, mates," Horace said to the policemen.

Jasper smiled at them. "Much obliged."

The paddy-wagon doors closed. Only then did Jasper and Horace see their fellow occupant. The top of his hat was chewed away. His pants were torn. Lionel Skinner's lip was bloody, and his wounded, throbbing ankles were wrapped in handkerchiefs.

Cruella cursed as she ascended from the barn cellar. She was covered in molasses. With every step, her shoes made a sloppy, sucking noise. She wiped her face with the back of her hand. Her eyes were rabid, her lips curled back in a ferocious snarl.

She marched forward and planted her soggy feet on the floor of the barn. "You beasts! You've won the battle but I'm about to win the wardrobe!" she said furiously to the animals. "My spotty puppy coat is in plain sight and leaving tracks. In a few moments I shall have what I came for while you will end up as sausage meat! Cruella De Vil has the last laugh!" she concluded.

In his stall, Punch suddenly reared up on his hind legs and battered his hooves on the floorboard where Cruella stood. It loosened, flew up, and sent her vaulting into the air.

She arced over the loft, shattered the window, and landed in a dung heap, which erupted with squealing pigs.

Police cars surrounded the Panther De Vil. A police officer stepped forward and shone his flashlight into the dung heap. "Ms. De Vil?"

Cruella's head emerged from the muck. "Yes?"

The officer tried not to smile. "We have a warrant for your arrest."

The farmyard animals erupted into a jubilant chorus of whinnies, caws, cackles, and oinks.

Lights flashed, sirens wailed, and radios barked out commands in a small village nearby. The police officers had found Pongo, Perdy, and the puppies.

We made it to the first village! My new puppies were introducing themselves to Perdy and me. Some had been stolen at birth and didn't have a name. We had to think of names for the orphan pups. I was just wondering how I could remember them all, when my thoughts were interrupted with the loud sirens of police cars coming toward us.

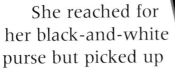

In the paddy wagon, an enraged Cruella sat next to Mr. Skinner. I've never met more incompetent boobs than you three."

She reached into her coat pocket and took out a soggy pack of cigarettes. Angrily, she threw them on the floor. "My business, my reputation, my life have been ruined because you fools got outsmarted by a pack of puppies . . ."

She reached for her black-and-white purse but picked up the skunk instead. "You call yourselves men. Ha!"

Still not noticing what she was doing, Cruella grabbed the skunk's tail as if it were a purse flap. "You're no better than the dumb animals who got the better of you," she sneered.

She glanced down, looking for a new pack of cigarettes. The skunk fixed her with a clear-eyed stare. Her mouth dropped open. Mr. Skinner, Jasper, and Horace gasped.

The skunk expelled its foul-smelling mist all over Cruella.

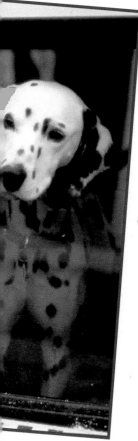

CHAPTER 16

One Big Happy Family

"**T**hey're here! Hurry!" Nanny cried at the living-room window.

Roger and Anita hurried out. Pongo, Perdy, and the puppies hopped out from the police car and scrambled toward them.

"Pongo, old boy! Perdy!" Roger cried joyfully as he gave Pongo a hug.

"The puppies!" Anita cried, her arms held open to receive them.

"The puppies, indeed!" Nanny echoed.

Roger turned to the policemen. "Thank you, gentlemen. We'll be forever grateful."

The policemen tipped their hats, got into their car, and pulled away. As Roger and Anita began to herd the puppies into the house, another police car pulled up.

Roger and Anita exchanged puzzled glances. Nanny tapped Roger on the shoulder and pointed down the street.

A line of police cars extended around the corner. Out of each car scrambled dozens of yipping Dalmatian puppies.

"We can't. We don't have room," Anita said. "Roger, please."

Roger was smiling. "We'll work something out. We'll get a bigger place."

Coming home was a glorious moment. Roger and Anita were so pleased to see us that they didn't seem to mind about our newly adopted extended family. Nanny wept with relief. All the puppies bounded about, playing happily.

That evening, I explained to Perdy that when Anita became pregnant, Roger changed two and two from four into five.

Now, five and five makes ten. So if you think about it really hard you might sometimes get another one, which makes ten plus one more.

101

Quite simple, really!

One hundred and one very happy Dalmatians . . .

As the puppies scrambled into the house, Roger picked up the newspaper. There was Cruella—her hair coated with molasses and dung, her clothes torn and filthy—on the front page.

A slow smile spread across his face. He had a wonderful idea, one that would end all their problems.

Anita and Roger sat at the table in the video-game-company office and watched Herbert play Roger's new game while Allan hovered nearby.

The little Dalmatian hopped across a creek and zoomed down a ravine as Herbert played with maniacal concentration.

Roger nudged Anita and pointed to the screen. Suddenly Cruella's face came up on the monitor. Her laughter echoed hideously.

Anita gasped. Outside, waiting on the terrace with the other puppies, Wizzer's ears shot up in surprise.

"Cool," said Herbert approvingly.

Squealing and yipping in fear, the puppies on the terrace fled.

Allan glanced at Herbert. The kid nodded, hopped

down from his chair, and picked up his book bag. "Get out your checkbook," he ordered. He looked over at Roger. "Excellent villain, mate."

"Congratulations," Allan said. "Let's go to my office."

As they left for Allan's office, Wizzer's head popped up in the open window. He trotted over to the television, where Cruella's face was frozen on the screen. With his paw, he pressed the joystick. Cruella's image exploded. Wizzer wagged his tail and barked happily.

Many Dalmatians later . . .

It was a glorious spring day in the English countryside. The lawn was green and lush, the flowers in bloom. Anita sat with her baby daughter on her lap.

Roger and Anita, being very kind and intelligent humans, bought the old De Vil mansion and transformed it into a splendid Dalmatian dog house!

Our puppies and steppuppies grew into fine dogs. They too, in turn, fell in love with one another. They had puppies of their own. In a few short years, my name changed from Pongo to Grandpa Pongo to Great-grandpa Pongo to Great-great-grandpa Pongo! We became a dynasty of Dalmatians—which means a family that goes on . . . and on . . . and on . . . and on. . . .

"**I** can hardly believe it," Roger said happily. "The baby's a year old. We have a new house. A new life."

"We have each other," Anita said softly.

"We have Nanny," Roger added.

"And I have the two of you," Nanny said proudly.

"We have two wonderful dogs." Roger nodded to Pongo and Perdy.

"And their children." The puppies, now grown, gathered around Anita and her baby.

"And their step-children." Nanny gestured to the one hundred and one Dalmatians.

"Look at them," Nanny said, pointing to the lawn.

A thousand puppies ran wild on the grounds of the former De Vil mansion. Roger and Anita had gutted it, restored it, and even painted the outside. It was now white—with black spots.

"Roger, darling." Anita patted her belly. "I have some wonderful news . . ."